"This is awesome!" Joe cried.

The pitching machine clicked. The ball shot out.

Joe swung the bat and hit the ball. Then David ran to catch it. The next ball dropped down and Joe swung again. Then Joe and David switched places.

Wishbone's ears suddenly pricked up.

"The pitching machine sounds funny!" he said.

David hit another ball, but before he could prepare for the next one, the machine pitched again. And again!

"There's something wrong," David said. "It's speeding up!"

Joe ran toward the machine. He ducked as a ball flew at him.

"It's gone crazy!" Wishbone said.

The Sorcerer's Apprentice

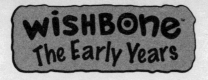

The Sorcerer's Apprentice

by **Carla Jablonski**
WISHBONE™ created by Rick Duffield

SCHOLASTIC INC.
New York Toronto London Auckland Sydney
Mexico City New Delhi Hong Kong

ISBN 0-439-12836-6

Copyright © 1999 by Big Feats! Entertainment, L.P.
All rights reserved. Published by Scholastic Inc., 555 Broadway,
New York, NY 10012, by arrangement with Lyrick Publishing™.

12 11 10 9 8 7 6 5 4 3 2 1   9/9 0 1 2 3 4/0

Printed in the U.S.A.   40

First Scholastic printing, October 1999

Edited by Pam Pollack
Copy edited by Jonathon Brodman
Continuity editing by Grace Gantt
Cover design by Lyle Miller
Cover painting and interior illustrations by Kathryn Yingling

For Matthew and Michelle,
who know all about softball and magic

The Sorcerer's Apprentice

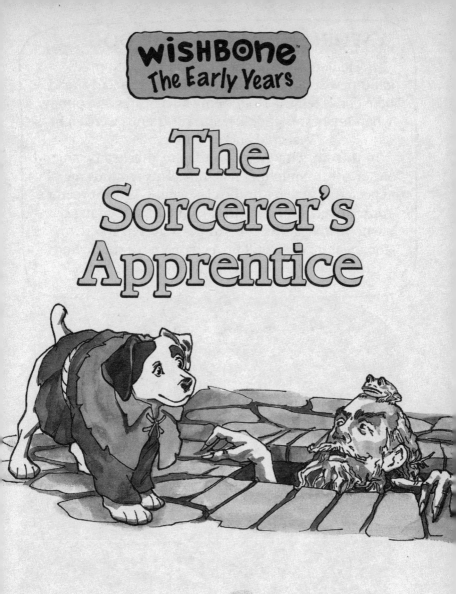

A WORD FROM OUR TOP DOG . . .

Helllooo! Wishbone here. Welcome to my
brand-new series of books, Wishbone: The Early Years.
These books tell the story of my adventures as a puppy,
when my best friend, Joe, and his friends were eight
years old and in third grade.

In this story my friends and I are attacked by an
out-of-control pitching machine. This reminds me of
the powerful sorcerer in the classic tale, **"The Sorcerer's
Apprentice."** I imagine that I am Philip, a young boy
who matches wits with an evil sorcerer. You're in
for a real treat, so pull up a chair, grab a snack, and
sink your teeth into *The Sorcerer's Apprentice!*

Chapter One

Play Ball!

"**R**eady, Joe?" David Barnes called from the middle of his backyard. He held up a softball.

Joe Talbot stood a few yards away. He held the bat tightly, then nodded. "Ready!"

David pulled back his arm—then let the ball fly!

C-r-a-a-c-k!

The sound of the bat hitting the ball made Wishbone's ears stand up. "Great hit, Joe! Look out, Joe DiMaggio!" Wishbone cheered.

Wishbone leaped up to chase the ball.

1

He moved so fast that he was a white-with-brown-and-black-spots blur.

Wishbone was a Jack Russell terrier puppy. His best human friend, Joe, was eight years old. David was the same age. Wishbone lived with Joe and Ellen Talbot, Joe's mom. David lived with his mom, dad, and baby sister next door to the Talbots. Joe and David were best friends.

Racing after the ball, Wishbone heard Joe call his name. *He must be cheering me on,* the puppy thought.

Wishbone reached the ball and grabbed it in his teeth. A moment later David caught up to him and quickly took the ball from him.

"Wishbone!" Joe said.

"What?" the terrier replied. "I got it as fast as I could."

The next time Joe hit the ball, Wishbone was in just the right spot as it hit the ground.

"How wath thath, Joe?" Wishbone said, with the ball firmly in his mouth.

This time, when David reached for the ball, Wishbone held it tightly in his teeth. Tug-of-war was one of his favorite games.

"Wishbone!" David said.

"Wishbone!" Joe repeated, running up to the dog.

A pair of hands grabbed Wishbone. He felt himself rise. His paws dangled a few feet above the ground.

"Have we been cleared for takeoff, Joe?" Wishbone licked the boy's nose.

Joe laughed. "No dogs allowed on this team."

"What!" Wishbone replied. "No dogs? You're playing ball, and you don't want an expert on the team? That doesn't make any sense."

Joe put Wishbone back on the ground. He pointed to the Barnes's back door. "Go back to the dugout, boy."

"But what am *I* going to do?" Wishbone asked, as he watched Joe walk away. "You don't even know how much you need me on the team."

The puppy lay on the ground. He rested his head on his front paws.

A moment later, the back door opened. David's dad, Nathan Barnes, poked his head out. "Ready for a snack?" he asked.

The terrier jumped up and twirled. "Oooh, you said the magic word!"

Joe and David looked at each other. They both shook their heads.

"No, thanks, Dad," David said. "We want to keep practicing."

"Can't we do both?" Wishbone asked. "Practice *and* snack?"

"The game is tomorrow," Joe said. "We want to be ready."

"I don't know, Joe," Wishbone said. "I think we need more practice snacking!"

Joe still didn't hear him. *I can't wait until I'm a full-grown dog,* Wishbone thought. *Then they'll listen to me.*

"Okay," Mr. Barnes said. "I'll be in the house if you need me." He went inside.

"Now it's my turn to pitch to you," Joe told David.

"Deal." David handed Joe the ball. Joe smacked it into his glove.

David picked up the bat Joe had dropped. He got into position.

Joe took a few giant steps away from

David. He turned, took aim, and pitched. The ball cracked off the bat.

Joe raced after the ball. David ran toward first base.

The puppy ran after the ball, too. He dashed between Joe's legs.

"Hey—" Joe yelled. He stumbled and fell down.

"Gotcha!" Wishbone grabbed the ball in his teeth. He trotted proudly in front of Joe.

"Wishbone, what did I tell you?" Joe said.

David laughed. He held out his hands to Wishbone. "Come on, boy. Give me the ball."

"You sure you want it back?" Wishbone asked. "I already picked the perfect spot to bury it." Wishbone put the ball down and started to dig.

David took the ball from Wishbone.

I'll have to pay close attention to this

game, Wishbone thought. *It should come with an instruction book.*

Joe took his place at bat. David pitched the ball.

Crack! The ball went sailing.

Wishbone raced after the ball. "I got it! I got it! I got it!" The ball landed a few inches in front of him. He picked it up in his mouth.

Joe and David clapped. "Way to go, Wishbone!" Joe cried. "You don't want to stay in the dugout, do you?"

"Too bad Wishbone can't pitch," David said with a laugh. "Then we could get in some *real* practice."

"Who says I can't pitch?" Wishbone sat back on the grass. "Is that another rule?"

The boys began to walk across the lawn. The puppy followed them.

"What if we had one of those pitching machines that pro players use?" Joe said.

"Those are cool," said David.

"Awesome," Joe agreed. "But nobody has his own."

"Hmm . . ." David stopped short.

Wishbone bumped into David's leg. "Hey, David. Aren't you supposed to signal when you come to a short stop?"

David reached down and gave Wishbone a pat. "Sorry, Wishbone. I guess I should have given you some warning."

"That's what I just said." The terrier licked David's hand.

David turned to Joe. "I think I know how we could make one of those pitching machines. There's some stuff in the garage that we could use."

Joe smiled. "Great!"

David grinned. "We'll be champs in no time."

"Oh, good! We're going to make a pitching machine," Wishbone said. Then he stopped and sat down. "Uh . . . what's a pitching machine?"

Joe and David slapped high-fives. "And if it's one of your inventions, it will work like magic!" said Joe.

The two boys hurried to the garage.

"I can hardly wait!" Wishbone said, as he trotted after the boys.

Hmm . . . magic, Wishbone thought. *That reminds me of a story. It's a fairy tale that has been told in many countries for many years. It's the tale of a young boy who learns about magic firsthand when he becomes the Sorcerer's Apprentice.*

Chapter Two

Into the Woods

Wishbone here! Did you know that the same fairy tale is sometimes told all over the world? Parts of the tale may change here and there, but the basic story stays the same. That's what it's like with the story of the Sorcerer's Apprentice. The tale has been told in countries as far apart as Israel, England, and Germany.

This version of "The Sorcerer's Apprentice" is based on the one that was written down by the famous Brothers Grimm. They put into book form some of the world's best-known fairy tales. They called their version of the fairy tale "The Magician and His Pupil."

Wishbone shut his eyes. He imagined himself in another time and in another place. He pictured a world with kings and queens and castles. Magic was around every corner. He saw a land where a young pup went out into the world to make his fortune. Soon Wishbone imagined himself as Philip, a young boy. He was homeless and on his own in the world for the first time.

Philip sniffed the fresh morning air. He stood in the middle of a busy cobblestone street wondering which way to go. He tried hard to stay out of the way of all the horses and wagons riding nearby.

Philip had come to town to look for a job. He had no family. He had to find a place to stay where there was a warm fire and regular meals. The best way for a young boy on his own to do that was to become someone's helper, or apprentice. As an apprentice, he would learn a trade. After a few years of training, he could get a good job.

If only someone would hire me, Philip thought. *I know I would do a good job. Wait until I prove what a hard worker, good jumper, great fetcher—*

Philip's thoughts were cut off by the sound of horses behind him.

"Yikes!" Philip leaped out of the way. A huge wagon rolled past. Big, shiny copper pots and pans banged against the sides of the wagon. Mud splashed onto Philip's mostly white fur.

"What this town needs is for someone to control the traffic!" he shouted at the driver of the wagon.

He rubbed off the mud as best he could. He even tried shaking some off. Luckily, the worst blotches matched his spots.

"Now, which way should I go?" He lifted his nose high into the air. His whiskers twitched. "Yum! I smell meat!"

With his tail wagging, Philip followed the tempting aroma. Soon he came to the very center of town.

"Market day!" he cried.

The main town square was crowded—with people, animals, and carts. It was market day. Folks from far and wide came to sell the things they made and the crops they grew on their farms. They brought everything to town by horse and wagon. They laid out their goods for sale on big wooden tables and counters.

"I should be able to find a master here to hire me," Philip said. The young boy followed his nose until he came to a large roasting pit.

"Excuse me," Philip said to the fellow turning the spit, which was the iron rod that held the meat in place over the fire. "I am looking for a job."

The man was very short and round, with several chins. "Well, what can you do, lad?" the man asked.

"I can do any job you give me!" Philip said eagerly. *Maybe I could be chief food taster,* he thought. *It's a tough job, but someone's got to do it.*

The man placed a big, heavy metal

platter on the counter near him. The platter was piled high with huge chunks of freshly cooked meat. "Well, my boy, you would have to turn the spit. . . ."

Philip's mouth watered at the thought. "I can do that!" Philip said happily. He eyed a piece of juicy meat.

"Help yourself." The round man nodded at the platter.

Philip reached out and grabbed hold of a freshly roasted piece of meat. He held it firmly between his paws and chewed noisily.

"You would also have to keep an eye on the fire. Make sure it stays hot."

Philip stopped chewing for a moment. "Sounds fine!" Then he finished the meat. He licked his chops. He eyed another juicy piece. He took it from the platter and gobbled it down in two bites.

This is my dream job, he thought. *Great food—and plenty of it.* He moved on to his third helping.

The man gulped in surprise. His eyes opened wide.

"So when do I start my work?" Philip asked.

"You don't," the man answered.

"Vhy noth?" asked Philip, his mouth full of more meat. He was trying to say "Why not?"

"You'll eat me out of business." The man laughed. He pulled the platter out of Philip's reach.

Philip turned and went on his way through the market. He walked between rows of heavy wooden tables piled high with goods for sale. He talked to many tradesmen, but no one needed an apprentice. Darkness was beginning to fall.

Philip shivered from the tip of his black nose to the end of his white tail. He worried that it would soon be nighttime and he would have nowhere to sleep.

He came to a blacksmith's table. The

blacksmith had his back to Philip. He held an iron poker into a glowing red fire.

"Excuse me. I'm looking for a job," said Philip. "Do you need an apprentice?"

"Why, yes!" the young blacksmith said as he turned around. "My last apprentice quit."

"Perfect!" Philip said. "I'm a very able worker."

The blacksmith smiled at Philip. At that moment, he accidentally knocked the hot poker into a stack of freshly made horseshoes.

"Yikes!" Philip leaped out of the way of the falling iron horseshoes. They clattered loudly onto the ground.

"Sorry! Sorry! I sure am clumsy," the blacksmith said. He bent down to pick up the horseshoes. The burning-hot poker missed Philip by only inches! It came close enough to heat up his fur!

I'm outta here! Philip thought. *It's too dangerous in this place.*

"Uh . . . I don't think this job is for me," Philip said. He backed away slowly from the blacksmith. He wanted to keep an eye on the man—and the fiery-red poker. That seemed like the safest thing to do.

"Come back! Please!" The blacksmith waved at Philip. The young man banged the hot poker into a pile of heavy copper kettles. They crashed onto the ground next to the fire, sending sparks flying. "I can teach you a lot!"

"No, thanks. I already know how to call the fire department." Philip turned and ran away from the blacksmith.

Philip left the market area. Soon he found himself at the edge of some woods. He sat down on the cool ground to figure out what to do next.

Suddenly, his muscles tensed. He smelled something.

"Cat!" cried Philip. He spun around.

A small black cat hissed at Philip.

"That's rude," said Philip.

The cat's fur stood on end. It raced past Philip. He chased the cat into the woods.

Soon, Philip was deep in a thick forest. The cat was gone, and Philip was lost.

Philip's nose twitched. He sniffed the air around him. He didn't recognize a single smell. It was almost as dark as midnight in the woods.

Philip then sniffed the ground around him. *Could this be a path? It smells as if people walked through here,* he thought. *I guess I'll follow it.*

Bushes with sharp thorns scratched him. Tiny lights glowed all around him. "Those look a lot like eyes!" Philip said. "Hundreds of eyes!"

Not one glowing eye blinked.

"Yeow!" A broken twig dug into his paw. Philip sat down and licked the sore spot. "Oo-kay, I'm ready for this adventure to be over now."

He shivered under his fur. *It's so dark. How long have I been in these deep woods?*

What will I do if I don't find my way? he worried. *I'm hungry. I'm tired. I'm lost.*

Philip was scared. The dark night, the forest—they seemed so *big* and endless. Philip suddenly felt very small.

Then he leaped up and shook his furred body hard. He barked loudly in all directions. *Just in case anyone out there sees me and thinks I'm afraid.* Philip started walking again.

The trees were even thicker and taller in the next part of the forest. "Trees are at the top of my list of favorites," Philip said. "But this is too much!"

Suddenly, he heard a noise high up in the trees above him. *What was that? Could it be the cat that got me into this mess?* Philip ran after the creature. *Maybe the cat can show me the way out of the forest.*

"Hey!" cried Philip.

He tripped over a bump in the ground. Pushing aside some leaves with a paw, he saw a large metal ring.

"This looks like a door handle," Philip said. He pushed away more leaves. It was a door made of rough wooden boards!

Why would there be a door in the ground in the middle of the woods? he wondered. *This must be the entrance to someone's cellar. But where's the house?*

All he saw around him was darkness and trees. The cat was nowhere in sight.

But something else was. Smoke!

A puffy cloud of gray smoke was floating out of the big tree in front of him. There was a twisted stone chimney sticking out of the huge tree trunk.

Someone must live inside this tree! But who . . . or what? Philip raced around to the other side of the tree.

"Yes!" he cried. There was a door in the trunk, although it was almost hidden.

Philip sniffed at the door. It smelled . . . strange.

He saw odd carvings in the tree bark. They were scary animals Philip had never seen—not even in books. There were also words and symbols he didn't know.

Nothing about this place seems friendly, Philip thought. *Should I knock?*

Then he thought, *Maybe I should. I have to ask for directions, anyway. Maybe I could even get a snack here.*

Philip reached out and scratched at the

door. Slowly, *very* slowly, the door opened with a *C-R-E-A-K!*

Suddenly, the body of an old man filled the doorway. He wore a robe of rough fabric that was the same brown-gray color as the tree trunk. His long white hair was tied back with a vine. Twigs stuck out of his flowing white beard.

"Who is that? I cannot see you in the darkness," the man said. His voice creaked like the door.

Philip put on his most polite expression. It usually won him a snack or two. "I was walking in the woods—"

"Why were you in the woods?" The old man's creepy-looking yellow eyes narrowed. His eyes were just like the cat's Philip had seen earlier. The way the man was staring at Philip made him shiver under his fur.

"I was looking for a job, and—" Philip said weakly.

"Well, well, well . . ." The man bent

down and studied Philip. "I might have one for you. I am working on something . . . big. It would help to have someone to take care of the chores I need done."

Philip began to wag his tail slowly. "Really?"

The man looked Philip directly in the eye. "First you must answer a question. Can you read?"

Philip wagged his tail even harder. "Oh, yes!" He loved to read.

The man stood quickly. He started to slam the door against Philip's muzzle. "Then this is no job for you."

"Wait!" Philip pushed his paw into the crack of the mysterious door. "Ooow . . . that hurts!" Philip said, as the door pressed against his paw. *This man is strange. But any job with him would be better than walking through the scary forest.*

The old man opened the door a few more inches. He looked down at Philip.

"Did you say *read?* Oh . . . no, no, no." Philip tried to laugh. "I thought you said *eat*. I am an excellent eater, but I cannot *read* at all."

The old man stroked his long, untamed beard. A spider crawled out of it.

Philip watched the spider and thought, *There's something you don't see every day.*

"Well, then," said the old man, "come inside. The job is yours." He opened the door wide.

"Thanks!" Philip said. *I think.*

The man turned and stepped deeper inside the tree trunk that was his house. Philip followed him inside. *I'd better keep my eyes and ears wide open,* Philip thought. *This is one strange guy.*

Chapter Three

The Sorcerer's Tree House

If it hadn't been for the round shape, Philip never would have guessed that he was inside a tree. He was standing in a great big round room with a stone floor and stone walls. *I don't think this is what most people mean by "tree house,"* he thought.

A huge oak table stood in the center. On one side of the room, glass bottles and jars sat in big wooden cabinets. The fronts of the cabinets were covered with more strange carvings.

On the other side of the room was a fireplace. A large pot bubbled over a fire there. Candles burned everywhere, sending ghostly shadows flickering across the walls.

"Nice place," Philip said. *If you like rooms designed in the style of the Late Weird period.*

The old man grunted.

Philip looked all around the strange house.

Near one end of the table, a stone staircase led upward, probably to a second level. Strange-looking dried plants hung from the wooden ceiling. Philip saw a trapdoor in the stone floor.

Rows of bookcases were built into the rounded walls. Philip wagged his tail wildly as he looked at all the books there. He loved books as much as he loved snacks.

The old man watched Philip carefully. His odd yellow eyes gleamed.

Philip's tail stopped in mid-wag. He suddenly remembered that he wasn't supposed to know how to read. "Uh . . . will it be my job to dust those books?" Philip asked.

"Yes," replied the old man. "And that is *all* you must do with them."

The man went over to the large oak table. A thick book lay open on it. Next to the book was a bowl filled with something smelly. The man slammed the heavy book shut. He dumped the foul stuff into the

fire. Sparks flew up. The odor got worse. Philip wondered if he would have to take care of the fire, too.

The old man grinned widely. It looked as if moss was growing right on his teeth. "It will be your job to watch the fire. It must always be lit."

Philip shivered. Was the old man able to read his mind?

"You will also do the washing up."

"Sounds good to me," Philip said. *As long as the food here isn't as bad as what was in that bowl.*

"You will sleep there," the old man said. He pointed to a small bed in a dark part of the room. Philip saw that the man's large, bony hand looked almost like an animal's claw!

"My room is upstairs," the man continued. Then he nodded at the trapdoor. "Below here is a storage room. No one is allowed down there but me. There are things below that must never see the light of day."

"Got it," answered Philip. *One less room to clean. This job is going to be easy.*

"What is your name, boy?" the old man growled.

"Philip."

"And I am Necromani."

"Nice to meet you." Philip held out a shaking paw.

Necromani gripped Philip's paw hard. His hand was ice-cold, and his fingernails were very sharp.

A short time later, Necromani filled a small iron pot with a thick vegetable stew. He set it over the fire to heat. When it was ready, the old man served it. Philip was surprised that it was quite tasty.

"I will tend to the outdoor garden by myself," Necromani told Philip. "There are plants that need special attention."

"Sure, boss!" Philip licked up the last bits of stew from his bowl. "So, what's this big project you're working on?"

33

Necromani slammed his fist down hard on the oak table. He hit it with such force that all the plates on it rattled. *"Never dare to question me about anything!"* he cried out in a booming voice.

"I-I'm sorry." Philip was so surprised that his fur stood on end. *He sure gets angry easily.* Then he reminded himself, *Be careful. You need this job. Don't get fired* before *the first day of your first job.*

Necromani leaned across the table. "As long as you follow all my instructions, we will get along fine," Necromani said. "But do not *ever* disobey me. You will regret it."

"I will obey," Philip promised.

"The most important thing is not to open a single book." Necromani's beady yellow eyes burned into Philip.

Philip shivered.

"Do you understand, boy?" Necromani boomed.

"Yessir," Philip said. He was scared, but

he already knew the first thing he wanted to do was to find out why all those books were so special to the old man.

Philip's answer seemed to please Necromani and calm him down.

"Yes," the old man said, slowly stroking his ragged beard. This time a little lizard slithered out. "I believe we will get along just fine."

The next morning Philip awoke early. He rolled over to one side of his little bed and peeked out of a hole in the tree. The sun was just coming up.

He sat up, stretched, and yawned. He didn't see Necromani anywhere.

Philip got out of his bed and then trotted over to a pile of logs. He dragged some to the fireplace. He got the fire going nicely. Then he noticed that the trapdoor was open. He slowly made his way over to investigate. *Necromani must be down there,* he realized. A strange odor drifted up from the storage room.

Philip's ears pricked up. He could hear Necromani climbing up the wooden ladder. Philip jumped back from the trapdoor. He didn't want Necromani to catch him nosing around.

Necromani's head came through the opening at the trapdoor. A frog was sitting on his wild gray hair. It leaped down and disappeared back into the shadows of the storage room. Philip thought the frog looked terrified.

Necromani climbed the rest of the way out, carrying a basket made of twisted vines. It was filled with slimy, smelly plants. He dropped the basket onto the big oak table. Several worms slithered out.

"Go crush all of these plants, boy. Then bring them to me."

Philip took the basket. He tried not to breathe in too deeply. *What is Necromani going to do with all this smelly stuff?* Philip wondered. But he got right to work. He was eager to show his new master what a good assistant he could be.

Late in the afternoon, Necromani went outside to work in his mysterious garden.

"Clean up the place while I'm gone," Necromani said. He left Philip alone in the tree house.

"Hmm . . . clean up," Philip said to

himself. "Well, dusting the books is one of my jobs."

Philip trotted over to the bookcases. He ran a cloth over the books.

"Let's see . . ." He read the titles out loud as he dusted. Some of them were hard to pronounce. "*The Encyclopedia of Spells, The Sorcerer's Dictionary, The Complete Book of Charms and Potions.*"

Philip gasped. Now he knew who his new master was. A sorcerer! Someone who makes things happen with magic spells!

"And that makes me . . ." Philip said slowly, ". . . a sorcerer's apprentice!"

 Wow! Philip had gone looking for a job—and he's ended up finding that, plus an unexpected adventure. Things are about to get exciting in Oakdale, too!

Chapter Four

The Perfect Pitcher

The puppy followed Joe and David into the garage.

"I bet I can find everything we need to make a pitching machine right in here," David said.

"Cool," Wishbone said. "I've always wanted to sniff around some more in here."

The walls of the garage were lined with shelves. Tools hung from pegboards.

David looked slowly around the garage. "There it is." He walked over to one corner and then pulled out an old leaf blower. "My father just bought a new leaf

39

blower," he explained. "He won't mind if we use this one. I think if we take off the end tube of the blower and add a T-shaped tube, it should work."

"I get it!" Joe exclaimed. "The blower will pitch the balls to us."

David grinned. "Yeah," he said.

"We just need something to feed the balls into the tube," Joe said.

"Speaking of feeding, Joe. . ." Wishbone rolled over. "Look how cute the puppy is. Isn't it time for a treat? Joe? Oh, Joe?"

Joe is really into this project, Wishbone realized. He scrambled back up to his paws and rubbed his nose across Joe's sneakers.

Joe held up the leaf-blower tube. Wishbone knew the machine worked like a vacuum cleaner—but the air blew in the opposite direction.

"How are we going to get the balls into the tube?" Joe asked.

David scratched his head. "Let me find a T-shaped tube, and I'll show you. I know there is one around here. My dad never throws out anything."

"Just my kind of guy," said Wishbone. "Only he should do what I do—bury the stuff. It gives it more flavor." He sat back down. He placed a paw on Joe's leg. "Hey, Joe! When do we get back to the playing part of the afternoon?"

"I think I found something that will work!" Joe said. He held up a T-shaped pipe and showed it to David.

David took the pipe. "It looks like it's the right size. Let's see if it fits."

David unscrewed the end of the tube from the leaf blower. Joe attached the T-pipe to the blower. One part of the T stood straight up.

It fit!

"We just need some duct tape to keep this on," David said. He went to the work

41

table and came back with wide, silver-colored duct tape.

Just then, Mr. Barnes walked in. "What are you doing, boys?"

Suddenly, David looked guilty. "We're building a pitching machine."

Mr. Barnes gave David a serious look. "Look, David, you know I like to encourage your projects, but you can't work with power tools on your own."

"I know. I'm sorry, Dad," David said.

Mr. Barnes looked at his son for a moment and smiled. "Just come to me for help next time." The man turned to the leaf blower. "You're using the leaf blower to pitch the balls. That's a good idea."

"And we're going to feed the balls in with this T-shaped tube," David said.

"It looks like that might work. Let's try it out." Mr. Barnes helped David tape the T-pipe in place. Then they all went outside.

Mr. Barnes put the leaf blower on the

grass. He made sure the T-pipe was well attached to the leaf blower.

"Can we try one, Dad?" David asked.

"Sure." Mr. Barnes smiled. "Until we see if this works, let me handle the blower. For safety, I'll leave the leaf blower on the ground. I'll point it away from us, also."

Mr. Barnes held the top of the T steady. He flipped the switch. The motor of the leaf blower roared into action. Joe dropped the softball down into the T.

Whoosh! The ball flew out the other end of the pipe. It rolled along the grass.

"It works!" David cheered.

"You did it!" Joe shouted.

Wishbone charged after the rolling softball. He grabbed it in his teeth. Then he trotted back to David, Mr. Barnes, and Joe. *"Vhavid,"* Wishbone said. "Blech!" he added, spitting out the ball. "David, just don't invent a machine that fetches the balls. I'll be out of a job."

"Someone will have to drop the balls into the T," said Joe.

David snapped his fingers. "Hey, Dad, I have an idea." He turned to Joe and said, "This will take a few minutes."

David motioned to his dad. The two went into the garage. Joe rolled a ball to Wishbone for a while. David and Mr. Barnes came back out twenty minutes later. David carried a five-gallon plastic water jug with a hinged lid. There were softballs inside the jug.

Using more of the duct tape, David and his father attached the upside-down jug to the T-shaped pipe.

"We turned the jug upside down and made the opening wider. We put a new lid on. It has a hinge and a spring on it, so it will let only one ball go into the pitching machine at a time," David explained. "We cut out the other end so we can put more balls in the jug."

"Wow!" said Joe. "It's really going to work great."

"You got it!" David said.

"Have fun, boys," Mr. Barnes said. "This looks safe enough to leave you by yourselves. Your pitching machine is great. Just don't forget to practice your catching and throwing, too."

"We won't, Dad," David said.

As soon as Mr. Barnes went back into the house, the boys began to work on the machine again. They wanted it to be perfect.

"The height's still not right," David told Joe.

Joe snapped his fingers. "The lawn chair!" He ran over to get it. Then Joe picked up the blower and set it across the arms of the chair.

"Come on, guys," Wishbone urged. "Let's play."

"This will be so awesome," Joe said.

He and David studied the machine. They made some more adjustments.

"I think *now* it's ready," David said.

Joe picked up his bat.

David picked up his glove. He flipped the On switch of the leaf blower. *Vroom!* The motor kicked in. Then a ball shot out.

Crack! Joe hit the ball. A solid hit!

The machine was working!

It's like magic, Wishbone thought.

Magic. That made him think of the magician who lived deep in the woods . . . and his curious and adventurous apprentice.

Chapter Five

Spells and More Spells

It's me again—Wishbone! Joe and David have invented an exciting new machine. Meanwhile, back in the tree house, Philip has made his own amazing discovery!

Wow! Philip's heart began to race. *My new master is a sorcerer! That is very good . . . or very, very bad.*

Now Philip knew why Necromani didn't want a helper who could read. He didn't want anyone to learn that he was a sorcerer and read his magic spells. Philip eyed all the books.

Philip's ears pricked up. He could hear footsteps. *Uh-oh. Necromani is on his way back from the garden.*

Philip ran to the other side of the room. He didn't want Necromani to catch him anywhere near the special books.

But I plan to read every single one of those books, Philip thought nervously.

Necromani went out into the woods early the next morning. Philip waited until he could no longer hear Necromani's footsteps. Then he raced over to the bookcases.

He pulled a thick book off one shelf. He opened the heavy leatherbound cover with his nose.

"Okay, now let's see . . ." Philip said, as

he read. There were lots of good spells to choose from. "I know! How about a spell to help me clean up?"

He turned to the Table of Contents. His eyes roamed down the list. His tail wagged. He found just the spell he was looking for.

"Perfect!" he cried. "*Dust*. That job takes so long, and it always makes me sneeze." Maybe he would never have to dust again! That would be great.

He flipped to the page in the book that described what to do. He read over what he needed to make the spell.

"What a strange bunch of things," Philip said. "Six butterfly eyelashes. Three drops of lizard drool. And one mushroom picked in the middle of the night under a full moon."

Philip read the labels on the jars nearby.

"Let's see. . . . Mushrooms picked at dawn. Mushrooms picked at sunset. Ah, yes, here they are! Mushrooms picked at midnight!"

Philip carefully measured everything he needed into a big bowl.

He checked the book again. "Now I just have to say the magic words." He looked carefully at the fancy letters. "I hope I say these right."

He cleared his throat. Then he took a deep breath. He was a little nervous. He was about to try casting his first spell!

"Here goes!" He checked the spell one last time. Then he shut his eyes tight. He announced, "Eyeno. Lika. Dustee. Room."

Did it work? he wondered, as he opened one eye to look around. *Is the room dusted?*

He opened the other eye. "Oh, no!" he cried.

The spell hadn't worked! The room wasn't sparkling-clean. Instead, everything was covered in dust. Thick, gray, fuzzy, nose-tickling dust.

"Ah-ah-choo!" Philip sneezed loudly. "What did I do wrong?"

He sneezed again. And again.

"I don't understand!" he exclaimed. "That spell was supposed to make the dust *disappear*—not *appear!*"

Before Philip could figure out what happened, his ears pricked up. He could hear Necromani's footsteps. He had to put the book, jars, and bowl away—fast!

He shoved the book back into its spot with his nose. Then he put back the bowl and the jars.

He looked quickly at the labels. "Now I see my mistake!" he said. "These are mushrooms picked at midnight, all right. But they're not mushrooms picked in the middle of the night *during the full moon.*"

Philip knew he would have to be very careful if he wanted to be a sorcerer!

He hurried to the fireplace. He wanted Necromani to think he had been watching the fire. He looked around. Everything was back to normal in the tree house, except for the thick coat of dust.

Necromani entered, carrying a vine basket full of strange plants. "Ah-choo!" The sorcerer sneezed hard. A bat flew out of his nestlike hair, and three mice dropped out of his thick beard.

This house isn't the only thing in need of housekeeping, Philip thought. *Old Necromani could use a good scrubbing himself. And maybe he should have that beard checked for more bats.*

"You've fallen behind with the dusting, haven't you, lad?" Necromani raised a heavy white eyebrow.

"Er . . . yes, sir." Philip picked up a twig broom. "I'll take care of it right away."

Necromani glared at him. "It wouldn't be good if I found out that you were up to something tricky—like spying instead of cleaning, for example."

"Of course not," Philip said. He wagged his tail happily so that Necromani wouldn't know how scared he was.

Necromani grunted. Then he vanished through the trapdoor into the storage room.

Philip went to work cleaning. He did an extra good job. He didn't want Necromani to be angry with him. He swished the broom under a couch.

Clank! His broom banged into something. A metal box.

"That's strange," Philip said under his

breath. "This wasn't here yesterday." He crawled under the couch. He pushed the box out into the open. There was a label on it that read: THE PLAN. SPELL ONE.

The Plan? Philip sat and stared at the box. *I wonder what kind of plan Necromani has in mind. Whatever it is, he won't want me to know about it.*

Philip nosed the box back under the couch. He would find out more about this plan. And he would be very careful.

Later that day, Philip had a chance to practice magic spells again. Necromani went into town for market day. He wouldn't be back until very late.

Philip pulled another thick book from the shelf. He was going to get this magic stuff right!

He opened the book. This time he was going to start at the very beginning and work his way step by step to the end.

He spent the whole afternoon doing

easy spells. He learned how to tie shoelaces and how to stop and start the clock on the wall just by using magic words.

"These spells are boring," he said soon. He decided to flip toward the back of the book. The spells there were much more of a challenge. "Hey! This looks like fun." He read a spell that told how to turn plain water into water with fruit flavors. "All this practice has made me thirsty."

He trotted over to a row of jars.

"I need some worm juice. Then a bit of bug guts. Hmm . . . This sure doesn't sound very tasty to me."

Philip filled three cups with plain water. Then he set the cups on a large tray. Finally, he mixed the smelly stuff together in a small bowl.

Philip lifted the bowl. The foul odor went straight up his nose. Phew!

He poured the mixture around the outside of the cups. Then he said the magic words. "Rutee! Tutee! Fresh and fruitie!"

Philip's brown eyes widened.

"Wow! Each cup of water has turned into a different color!"

He lapped up the water in each cup.

"The red water is strawberry! The green water is lime! And the orange water is orange."

I did it! he thought, his tail wagging proudly. *I'm a sorcerer.* He leaped up and spun in the air.

He came down with a thud. "Wh-wh-?"

The whole room had changed! The walls were purple! The bookcases were orange! Philip glanced down and saw that his white fur was now blue!

"Oh, no! What am I going to do?" He quickly searched through the big book. "Oh, good," he said. He ran a blue paw along the words. "It says right here that the spell will wear off after an hour."

Philip hoped the book was right! How could he ever explain the multicolored room to Necromani? How could he explain his blue-colored fur? Luckily, Necromani wasn't due back for a few more hours.

Philip decided it was time to do his chores. Enough magic for one day.

"So I'm not a master sorcerer . . . yet!" he said, his tail wagging. "Hey, no one gets it perfect the first time!"

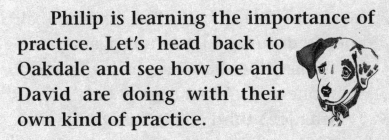

Philip is learning the importance of practice. Let's head back to Oakdale and see how Joe and David are doing with their own kind of practice.

Chapter Six

Out of Control!

"This is awesome!" Joe cried.

The leaf blower whirred. *Pop!* The softball shot out.

Joe swung the bat and hit the ball. David ran to catch it. The next softball dropped down and Joe swung again.

"A machine that plays ball with you," Wishbone said. "What a great idea."

After Joe's third out, it was David's turn to do some hitting. David ran toward Joe to get the bat.

A ball flew at them. David and Joe ducked low.

"The puppy has it!" Wishbone ran after the ball and grabbed it in his teeth.

"Whoops!" Joe said, laughing. "We forgot that the machine doesn't take time-outs!" He handed David the bat.

Before David got into position, another ball popped out at them. This one landed in their next-door neighbor's flower bed. It knocked over two petunias.

"Uh-oh," Joe said. "Miss Gilmore isn't going to be very happy about her flowers."

Then another ball shot by. Wishbone dropped the ball in his teeth. "Heads up!" he cried, as he chased the second ball.

"Whoa!" David exclaimed. He held up the bat. "I'd better start hitting!"

Crack!

"Good hit!" Joe raced to catch the ball. It dropped into his glove with a thud.

Wishbone's ears suddenly pricked up. "That pitching machine sounds funny!" he said.

David hit another ball, but before he could prepare for the next one, the machine pitched again. And again!

"Hey!" David cried. Two balls flew at him before he could move.

"What's going on?" Joe called.

"I think there's something wrong with the pitching machine," David said. "It's speeding up!"

"I knew it!" Wishbone barked at the machine. "Slow down!"

"You keep hitting," said Joe. "I'll try to fix it."

Joe dashed across the lawn.

"Yahh!" he shouted. He ducked as a ball flew at him. "Now it's pitching to me!"

"The pipe is flipping around after it shoots out a ball!" David realized.

"It's gone crazy!" Wishbone said. He watched as another ball dropped down. Sure enough, the pipe slid along the lawn chair. It sent the ball flying toward the house.

"We're going to be in big trouble if that machine breaks a window," David said.

"Uh-oh." Wishbone went over to the machine. He looked at it very carefully. "The hinge on the jug is stuck. The lid will not close! The spring must have come loose."

The machine spat out the balls faster and faster. And they went in all directions! Joe leaped this way and that to try to catch them. David hit them away from the house. The puppy jumped up and knocked them out of the way with his nose—when he could.

"That *hurts!*" Wishbone said.

"The machine has gone crazy!" David exclaimed. He swung and missed.

"It's out of control!" Joe agreed. He threw himself toward a ball.

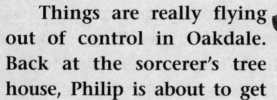

Things are really flying out of control in Oakdale. Back at the sorcerer's tree house, Philip is about to get some interesting surprises of his own.

Chapter Seven

The Terrible Plan

Several weeks went by. Philip kept practicing magic secretly. He also made sure to keep up with his chores. Sometimes while he cleaned, he found a new metal box hidden somewhere in the tree house. Each was labeled "The Plan," and each had a spell number on it. So far, Philip had found boxes up to Spell Six.

One morning Necromani sent Philip out into the woods with a basket. He was told to find lots of flowers, mushrooms, and moss. Necromani warned Philip that the job could take all day.

Philip's fine sense of smell helped him finish the work quickly. He sniffed out everything on his master's list in no time at all. "I think I have a nose for this," Philip said to himself as he headed home.

Philip stopped in his tracks in front of the tree house. His whiskers tingled. Something very strange was happening inside.

Blue smoke poured out of the chimney. There was electricity in the air. It made Philip's fur stand up.

"I don't know what Necromani is doing in there," Philip said. "But it's giving me a bad hair day."

Philip set down the heavy basket. He stood on his hind legs and pushed open the huge wooden door with both paws.

What a sight!

Necromani stood in front of the fire. His back was to Philip. He was wearing his big, bulky robe. He rocked back and forth on his heels. He chanted strange words—

words Philip had not read in any of the magic books.

Thick blue mist rose up from the big iron pot hanging over the fire. The mist was the same color as the smoke that Philip had seen coming out of the chimney outside. The flames shot high, almost covering the pot. Amazing! Tiny clouds floated inside the mist.

Suddenly, little thunderbolts burst out of the clouds!

Surprised, Philip let out a bark.

Necromani spun around. His sharp yellow eyes flashed like lightning!

"Why are you sneaking up on me?" the sorcerer shouted.

"I-I'm not," Philip said. "I finished picking all of the flowers and plants you wanted."

Necromani turned back around. He waved his hands over the fire. The mist disappeared. The fire shrank back down to its regular size.

"You left the fire too high," the sorcerer scolded. "That's what made all that blue smoke appear."

"B-but—" Philip began to disagree. Then he changed his mind. He knew Necromani would never admit that he was casting spells.

Philip thought about those little clouds for the rest of the day. How did

Necromani do it? What kind of spell was the magician working on? Philip had to find out if it was part of The Plan.

That night, Philip listened to Necromani snore upstairs. Once he was sure the sorcerer was asleep, Philip crept over to the bookcases.

Carefully, Philip pulled *The Encyclopedia of Spells* from a shelf. It was very heavy. He slowly laid it out on the floor. He nudged it over to the little patch of moonlight beaming in from a window.

"Okay, Necromani," Philip whispered to himself. "I'm going to find out just what you're up to."

He sat in front of the book and pawed from page to page. He found a picture that looked just like the mist and clouds he had seen earlier. His tail wagged with excitement.

"So what does this Storm Spell do?" he wondered. He read the spell.

Philip's eyes widened. "Oh, no!" He gasped. His heart thumped hard in his chest.

The Storm Spell was very powerful. A magician used it to control the weather.

"'In this way,'" Philip read from the book, "'the magician will be able to scare everybody in the land. People will do anything he wants. It is the final spell to use to take over an entire kingdom!'"

Philip sat up in shock as the truth hit him. *Necromani plans to use his powers to rule over everyone in the land! This must be The Plan. It looks as if he's up to the last part. Somehow I have to stop him!*

"What are you doing?" Necromani's booming voice startled Philip.

Philip was so scared that he froze over the book.

Necromani hurried down the staircase from his room. "What are you doing with my book?" He shouted so loudly that the jars on the shelves shook.

Philip thought fast. "I couldn't sleep," Philip explained to the old man. "So I thought I would pass the time by looking at some pictures."

He pointed to one of the drawings in the book. He hoped Necromani didn't notice his paws trembling with fear.

Philip faked a big yawn. "You know, it worked. I feel really sleepy now."

Necromani walked closer to Philip, staring at him. The magician's wild white hair nearly covered his wrinkled old face. Philip couldn't tell what the sorcerer was thinking.

I hope he believes me, Philip thought. *If not, I'm in big trouble.*

 **Back in Oakdale, Joe and David are in trouble, too. One of us had better come up with a plan—quickly.**

72

Chapter Eight

Wishbone to the Rescue!

"We're under attack!" Wishbone dove to the ground and rolled over. Softballs were flying everywhere.

The pitching machine whirred and roared. The pipe flipped and slid around wildly on the lawn chair. Balls were still dropping from the jug.

Pow! Pow! Pow! David cracked the balls with the bat.

Thwump! Thud! Thwump! Joe leaped and jumped to catch all the balls. Sweat poured down his face.

"We have to stop the balls from breaking

anything!" Joe shouted to David. "Keep hitting!"

"Incoming!" Wishbone cried out. He ducked under a fast-moving softball. It rolled under a bush.

"I don't know if I can keep hitting this fast!" David yelled to Joe.

Wishbone glanced over. David was breathing hard. He looked really tired.

Wishbone knew that he had to do something to help. But what?

"Okay, pitching machine," Wishbone growled, "it's either you or me."

The puppy planted his four paws firmly

on the ground. He gave the machine some warning barks. Then he leaped forward.

Pow! Out flew another ball. Wishbone dropped to the ground and rolled over.

"Ha! You missed me!" he shouted at the machine.

The puppy lay on the ground and studied it.

"If I can get to the back of the machine without it clobbering me, I should be able to reach the controls. I have to stop the machine! My friends need me! *I* need me!"

I have to stay low to the ground, Wishbone figured out. *Then I can crawl in under the line of fire. Maybe the machine won't notice my sneak attack.*

His belly nearly touching the ground, Wishbone crept forward. He could feel the grass rubbing against his fur. "Hey! That tickles! Keep going," the puppy told himself. "Joe and David are going to wear down before that machine does!"

He could hear David and Joe running all around him. Wishbone kept his eyes glued on the wild pitching machine. He held his nose to the ground. The balls flew over his head.

Inch by inch, paw by paw, Wishbone wiggled toward the machine. Yes! The leaf blower was almost within reach now. He could almost touch it.

But where is the switch that turns the thing off? he wondered.

Wishbone's ears pricked up. Now the machine was making loud grinding noises. *That can't be good*, he thought. The pipe bounced around, banging every which way on the lawn chair.

Crash!

"Yah!" Wishbone yelped. The jerking pipe knocked over the lawn chair! Now the balls were flying straight at Wishbone!

He had to flip the switch—now!

But where?

He reached out a paw . . . closed his eyes, and . . .

Whoa! There's trouble everywhere! Back in the tree house, Philip is having his own problems. Big ones!

Chapter Nine

Magic Against Magic

"**I**'ve caught you!" Necromani shouted. "I knew you could read!"

"Uh . . . uh . . ." Philip didn't know what to say. He backed away from Necromani. He bumped into the big oak table behind him.

"Do you think I am a fool?" Necromani's beady yellow eyes flashed like two bolts of lightning. "Did you think you could keep this from me?"

"No! Of course not!" Philip's heart banged in his furred chest. Terror made it hard for him to think.

"Now I must destroy you!" Necromani boomed. "No one may know my secrets!"

"I don't know anything!" Philip said. His four legs shook with fear. "Really! Just ask some questions. I won't know a single answer!"

"Silence!" Necromani held out his clawlike hands.

What is he going to do to me? Philip wondered. *Is he going to cast a horrible spell? Or will he break me in two with his bare hands?*

Philip wasn't going to wait to find out!

Philip shut his eyes. He tried hard to think of all the spells he had practiced the past weeks. *Can I save myself somehow?*

"Ieta! Lotsa! Werms!" Philip screamed.

The moment he said the magic words, Philip felt his body change. He got smaller and smaller. His nose grew longer and more pointy. All his fur fell off. He was covered in feathers, instead!

"I'm a bird!" Philip cried. "I turned myself into a bird!"

Necromani lay crumpled on the dirt floor. He had rushed toward Philip with his claws, reaching for him. When the sorcerer had missed his target, he crashed to the ground.

"You have to learn to be light on your feet," Philip told Necromani. "Like me!"

Philip flapped his new wings. He flew out of the tree house through a small hole in the wall.

He landed on a low branch outside. He couldn't believe it! He was a bird! *All that studying has paid off,* Philip thought.

At that moment, Necromani burst out of the door of the tree house. His angry yellow eyes locked on Philip.

"There you are!" Necromani snarled. "You'll never get away from me!"

Philip's eyes grew wider and wider as he watched Necromani. The magician began to change.

Necromani's wild hair and beard grew even longer. Quickly, he was covered in light-colored fur. Then it all darkened to a deep black. At the same time, the old man's body got smaller. But his shining yellow eyes never changed. And they never stopped staring right at Philip!

"Why, he's turning into . . . that black cat—that creature I chased a while back in the woods!" Philip gasped.

With a frightening yowl, the cat leaped

at Philip the bird. Philip was so shocked that he forgot to flap his wings. He fell off the branch and hit the ground with a thud.

The cat jumped down from the branch. It raised its paws. The claws looked very sharp.

"Wings, don't fail me now!" Philip flapped his wings hard. He rose from the forest floor. But flying was new to him, and he wasn't very strong. He landed on a branch to rest. The cat quickly climbed up beside him.

"This isn't working!" Philip said. *Turning into a bird was a bad idea,* he thought. *Cats eat birds. I'd better quickly try something else.*

He glanced around and saw the lake. *I know what I must do! Cats hate to get wet.*

Philip concentrated hard. He used his imagination to make a picture in his mind. Then he said some magic words. "Wishy! Washy! Wishy! Fishy!" He flew to the lake and fell into the water—as a fish!

The perfect escape! Philip thought. *That cat will never follow me into the water.*

"Well, Necromani always thought there was something fishy about me," Philip said. He tested his fins. He swam forward at top speed.

Splash! Suddenly, a gigantic yellow-eyed fish appeared right next to Philip.

"Why, Necromani, you look different!" Philip teased. "But I know you by those eyes."

Philip turned into a bigger fish. In a flash, Necromani turned himself into a net to catch his prey!

Necromani the net scooped up Philip the fish.

"Now what do I do?" Philip wondered. "I know!"

Philip imagined he was a pair of sharp scissors. Then he quickly said the words of the spell. "Flip! Dip! Snip! Snip!"

The next thing Philip knew, he was cutting his way out of the net.

"Oh, no! I'm sinking!" he cried.

The scissors splashed into the water and disappeared. Philip knew he had to change into something else. He quickly said the words of a spell that switched him back to a little fish.

"I wonder where Necromani is now." Philip swam around the lake. "Maybe when I cut apart the strings of the net, I made him disappear."

He came near a dark cave that overlooked the water. Sharp white stones hung down from the top of the cave opening. More pointy stones poked up from the bottom.

How weird, Philip thought. He swam over to the mouth of the strange cave. He started to swim inside to explore. Then he figured it out. *This isn't a cave at all! It's a giant mouth! And those aren't stones. They're deadly teeth!*

The little fish spun around. It swam as

fast as it could away from the big, open mouth. Necromani had turned himself into an alligator!

I have to get back on dry land, Philip told himself.

"See you later, alligator!" he shouted. He shut his eyes. He chanted the magic words. "Sea! Yalata! Al! Ligator!"

When he opened his eyes again, his skin was thick and scaly.

"I'm an alligator, too—and a big one!" *I guess I was thinking so hard about alligators that I ended up turning into one.*

Philip watched the yellow-eyed alligator crawl out of the lake. He knew that it was Necromani. Philip realized he was a bigger alligator than the sorcerer.

Philip opened his mouth wide, showing great, big, sharp, jagged teeth. He rushed toward the other alligator.

Necromani stared at him. Then the magician vanished!

"Where are you?" Philip cried. "What have you turned into now?"

Philip's alligator eyes searched all around the forest. He saw trees, birds, flowers, and rocks. He could not find Necromani. Philip was afraid the sorcerer would sneak up on him.

"I have to figure out what he changed into," Philip said. "I can't let him catch me in a surprise attack."

Philip stared closely at everything around him.

"Hey—what's that?" Philip noticed a grain of rice stuck in a crack in a rock. "How did that get there?"

He looked even closer. Yes! Two teeny-tiny yellow eyes stared back at him from inside the grain of rice. It was Necromani!

Philip opened up his big alligator mouth. His teeth clamped down hard on the rock.

"Ow!" The grain of rice was still stuck

in the crack in the rock. "My mouth is too big to get hold of that grain. Even if I turned back into myself, my paws would never be able to grab it. Necromani is very clever."

Philip flicked his scaly alligator tail.

"I just have to be *more* clever!" Philip said. In a flash, Philip turned himself into a rooster by saying the magic words, "Hudoo! Yudoo! Cockle-doodle-doo!"

Philip pecked at the crack in the rock with his sharp beak. It was easy to get hold of the grain of rice that way. He gobbled it down.

"I hope Necromani doesn't give me a stomach ache!" Philip the rooster crowed in laughter.

That was the end of the evil magician.

Philip turned back into himself. "I guess all my practice paid off. I'm glad I remembered a lot of the spells I read."

Philip trotted back merrily to the tree

house. *I'm going to study magic spells even harder now,* he thought. He wagged his tail happily.

"I'm going to learn so much that I'll write my *own* book of spells. It will be a best-seller!"

Philip spent the rest of his days learning more and more magic. He became known through-out the land as the kindest of all  sorcerers. For many years, people spoke of all his good and wondrous deeds.

Now, if I can only stop that wild pitching machine, maybe people will feel the same way about me in Oakdale.

Chapter Ten

Coach Wishbone

Wishbone flipped the switch with his paw. The machine clicked off. Balls still dropped down through the pipe. But without the leaf blower's power pushing them, they just piled up inside the tube.

"Way to go, Wishbone!" David cheered.

"You saved us, Wishbone!" Joe cried.

"I knew you needed me, Joe," Wishbone said, looking up at the boy. "Who says dogs can't play softball? I think it should be clear to everybody that you need a good coach." He looked at the pitching machine. "Not everyone on this team plays by the rules."

Joe flopped down onto the grass. "I feel so tired."

David dropped the bat. Then he lay on the lawn, too.

"I've never hit like that in my whole life," David said. "My hands hurt from holding the bat so hard."

"Let's lie here for a couple of minutes," Joe said.

"I'm all for naps!" Wishbone said. He curled up beside Joe.

"What went wrong?" David asked.

"I don't know," Joe said. "Do you think we'll be able to fix the machine in time to get in some more practice?"

"I hope so," David replied.

The back door opened. Mr. Barnes stepped outside. "Joe," he said, "your mom just phoned. She wants you to come home for dinner."

Wishbone leaped to his feet. "Dinner is even better than a nap!"

"Already?" Joe sat up slowly.

"David, come on in and wash up," Mr. Barnes continued. "It's time to set the table."

"But Dad," David complained. "We have to fix the pitching machine. We didn't have much time to practice with it."

"It will have to wait," said Mr. Barnes. "Joe's mom is expecting him. And your mom needs your help."

The two boys got up.

"Come on, Wishbone," Joe said. "I guess it's time to go home."

"I'm one step ahead of you," Wishbone said. He dashed toward the house he shared with Joe next door. He looked back. Joe and David were still talking. "Make that a whole lot of steps ahead of you."

David turned to go into his house.

Joe walked over to Wishbone. "I hope

we don't lose the big game tomorrow because of that machine," Joe said.

"Don't worry, Joe," Wishbone said to his friend. "You'll feel better once you get a nice big bowl of food in front of you. Dinner always cheers me up!"

The next day after the game, Wishbone wagged his tail very hard.

"We won!" the puppy cheered. He trotted behind Joe and David as they walked toward Ellen's car.

Joe and David's softball team won, 5–3. During the drive home, Joe and David couldn't stop talking. Their game had improved!

"I think that machine really helped us," Joe said.

David laughed. "I hit better today than before. I bet it was all that practice I got yesterday—trying to keep the balls from hitting me in the face!"

"That *was* hard!" Joe smiled. "Catching and fielding today were easy, after running after all those wild balls yesterday."

"That turned out to be the best pitching machine after all," David said.

"The best invention for practicing," Joe agreed. "Once we work on the machine and get it fixed, then we can have it whenever we want to practice."

Wishbone wagged his tail hard. "I had it figured that way the whole time," he said. "Just call me 'coach'!"

About "The Sorcerer's Apprentice"

The tale of a sorcerer being outsmarted by his student is a very popular one. There are almost as many versions of this story as there are countries in which it is read! The titles may change, but the plot remains basically the same. One of the fascinating aspects of fairy tales and folktales is that bits and pieces of different stories are often woven together to form a brand-new tale. The first half of the story may be attached to the second half of another story. Or details may change as the story travels from one culture to another. In the Israeli version of "The Sorcerer's Apprentice" (called "Pupil Who Excelled His Master"), the student turns into a ring and a peach. In the Arabic retelling (called "The Boy Magician"), the student turns into a razor and a dove.

Wishbone's version is inspired by a story collected by the brothers Jakob and

Wilhelm Grimm. It's called "The Thief and His Master." The Grimm brothers lived in Germany in the 1800s. They studied languages and mythology and even wrote textbooks on grammar. They were particularly interested in the folktales of their native country. They interviewed hundreds of people, gathering from them their favorite stories. They put these stories together in a book called *Household Tales*, which was published in 1812. It was a big hit, so they kept adding more stories and publishing new editions. The Brothers Grimm published a total of more than one hundred stories!

About Carla Jablonski

Carla Jablonski is an actress, director, and writer who lives in New York City. She is the author of two books in the WISHBONE book series: The Adventures of Wishbone *Homer Sweet Homer* (inspired by Homer's *The Odyssey*); and The Super Adventures of Wishbone *The Legend of Sleepy Hollow* (inspired by Washington Irving's classic tale). She has also written one Clueless book, *Southern Fried Makeover*. Carla has also edited many best-selling books for children, including titles by R. L. Stine, and books for the series Choose Your Own Adventure and The Hardy Boys Mystery Stories.